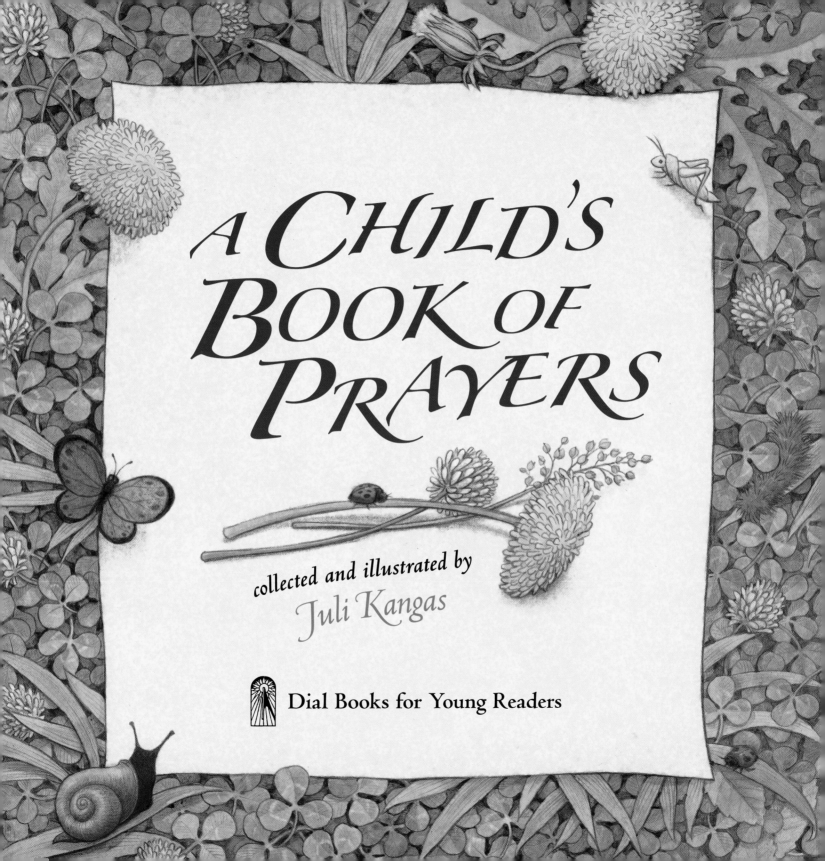

A CHILD'S BOOK OF PRAYERS

collected and illustrated by

Juli Kangas

Dial Books for Young Readers

Dedicated with love to Louise and George

DIAL BOOKS FOR YOUNG READERS
A division of Penguin Young Readers Group
Published by The Penguin Group
Penguin Group (USA) Inc., 375 Hudson Street, New York, NY 10014, U.S.A.

The publisher does not have any control over and does not assume
any responsibility for author or third-party websites or their content.

Designed by Nancy R. Leo-Kelly
Text set in Centaur MT & Zapfino initials
Manufactured in Mexico
ISBN-13: 978-0-8037-3054-0

The art was prepared using pencil, watercolor, and oil wash.

A Note About the Text

Many of the prayers and poems included here are unattributed; they have been passed down through the generations, and information about their original authorship has been lost. In the case of the poem on page 8, it has often been incorrectly attributed to Ralph Waldo Emerson, but its true author is unknown.

Lord, teach a little child to pray,
And then accept my prayer;
You can hear all the words I say,
For You are everywhere.
A little sparrow cannot fall
Unnoticed, Lord, by Thee:
And though I am so young and small,
You do take care of me.

Good morning, dear God,
I offer to You
My thoughts, words, and actions
And all that I do.

Dear Lord,
So far I've done all right.
I haven't lost my temper,
Haven't been greedy, grumpy, nasty, or selfish.
I'm really glad about that.
But in a few minutes, God,
I'm going to get out of bed.
And from then on,
I'm going to need a lot more help.

For every cup and plateful,
God make us truly grateful.

Dear Father, hear and bless
Thy beasts and singing birds,
And guard with tenderness
Small things that have no words.

For flowers that bloom about our feet,
Father, we thank Thee.
For tender grass so fresh, so sweet,
Father, we thank Thee.
For the song of bird and hum of bee,
For all things fair we hear or see,
Father in heaven, we thank Thee.

For blue of stream and blue of sky,
Father, we thank Thee.
For pleasant shade of branches high,
Father, we thank Thee.
For fragrant air and cooling breeze,
For beauty of the blooming trees,
Father in heaven, we thank Thee.

For this new morning with its light,
Father, we thank Thee.
For rest and shelter of the night,
Father, we thank Thee.
For health and food, for love and friends,
For everything Thy goodness sends,
Father in heaven, we thank Thee.

$\mathcal{G}$od bless the field and bless the furrow,
Stream and branch and rabbit burrow.
Bless the minnow; bless the whale.
Bless the rainbow and the hail.
Bless the nest, and bless the leaf.
Bless the righteous and the thief.
Bless the wing and bless the fin.
Bless the air I travel in.
Bless the mill and bless the mouse.
Bless the miller's red brick house.
Bless the earth, and bless the sea.
God bless you, and God bless me.

Lord, teach me all that I should know;
In grace and wisdom I may grow;
The more I learn to do Thy will,
The better I may love Thee still.

Isaac Watts

Thank you for the world so sweet,
Thank you for the food we eat,
Thank you for the birds that sing,
Thank you, God, for everything!

Edith Rutter Leatham

Let me walk with you
Although my steps are small.
Stay beside me . . .
Hold my hand . . .
And never let me fall.

I trust you, God, to take good care
Of people dear to me—
The ways You love and help us all
Are more than we can see.

All things bright and beautiful,
All creatures great and small,
All things wise and wonderful,
The Lord God made them all.

Each little flower that opens,
Each little bird that sings,
He made their glowing colors,
He made their tiny wings.

The tall trees in the greenwood,
The meadows where we play,
The rushes by the water
We gather every day—

He gave us eyes to see them,
And lips that we might tell
How great is God almighty,
Who has made all things well.

Cecil Francis Alexander

$\mathcal{B}$less the four corners of this house,
And be the lintel blessed,
And bless the hearth and bless the board,
And bless each place of rest.

And bless the door which opens wide,
To strangers as kin,
And bless each crystal window pane
That lets the sunshine in;

And bless the rooftree overhead,
And every sturdy wall—
The peace of man, the peace of God,
The peace of love on all.

Arthur Guiterman

Oh, the Lord is good to me,
And so I thank the Lord
For giving me the things I need,
The sun, the rain, and the apple seed.
Oh, the Lord is good to me.

Attributed to John Chapman, aka Johnny Appleseed

At the back of the bread is the flour.
At the back of the flour is the mill.
At the back of the mill is the wind
and the rain and the Father's will.

O God, make us children of quietness
and heirs of peace.

St. Clement

In gratitude we bow our heads
To thank Thee, Lord, for daily bread,
And may we use the strength it brings
For doing kind and helpful things.

Dear God,
Thank You for the food before us,
the friends beside us,
and the love between us.

Please give me what I ask, dear Lord,
If You'd be glad about it.
But if You think it's not for me,
Please help me do without it.

I pray that ordinary bread
Was just as nice as cake;
I pray that I could fall asleep
As easy as I wake.

God bless all those that I love.
God bless all those that love me.
God bless all those that love those that I love,
And all those that love those that love me.

From an old New England sampler

Two little eyes to look at God.
Two little ears to hear His word.
Two little lips to sing His praise.
Two little feet to walk His ways.
Two little hands to do His will.
One little heart to love Him still.

$\mathcal{D}$ear God, be good to me,
The sea is so wide and my boat is so small.

Traditional prayer of Breton fishermen

Now I lay me down to sleep,
I pray the Lord your child to keep;
May angels watch me through the night
And wake me with the morning light.

I see the moon.
The moon sees me.
God bless the moon,
And God bless me.

Good night! Good night! Far flies the light;
But still God's love shall flame above,
Making all bright. Good night! Good night!

Victor Hugo